To Adam, our sweetheart,
with love, hugs and kisses from
Mum, Dad, Harry, Robbie and Molly.

Adam is an angel and lives on a cloud
and makes his Mummy and Daddy so proud.
With long golden hair you just could not miss,
he always has time for a hug and a kiss.
The message he sends from his cloud every day,
is to spend more time with each other and play.
The most important thing in life is this,
show your love for your family with a hug and a kiss.

Written by Benji Bennett.
benji@adamscloud.com

Illustrations by Roxanne Burchartz.
www.roxanneburchartz.com

Designed by Bold.
www.reallybold.com

This 2018 edition printed in Ireland by Watermans Printers.
www.watermansprinters.ie

ISBN 978-1-906818-05-0

Published by

An imprint of Adam's Printing Press Publishing.

Adam's Cloud is dedicated to spreading Adam's message of the importance of love, laughter and play within the family
and will make a donation from the proceeds of all books published under its imprint to children's charities.

Adam's Cloud
PO Box 11379, Blackrock, Co. Dublin, Ireland.
Email: info@adamscloud.com
Web: www.adamscloud.com
Tel: +353 1 2833620

2% of the proceeds from the sale of this book will go to

Founded by Paul Newman in 1994, Barretstown exists to improve the quality of life of children with serious illness
by providing life changing programmes of therapeutic recreation which aim to rebuild their confidence, trust and self esteem.
Hospitals take care of the physical effect of serious illness; Barretstown helps to heal the emotional scars.

"I wonder what the most wonderful thing in this
Is it a wonderful person or place or a big

wonderful world could be,
buzzy bumbley bee?"

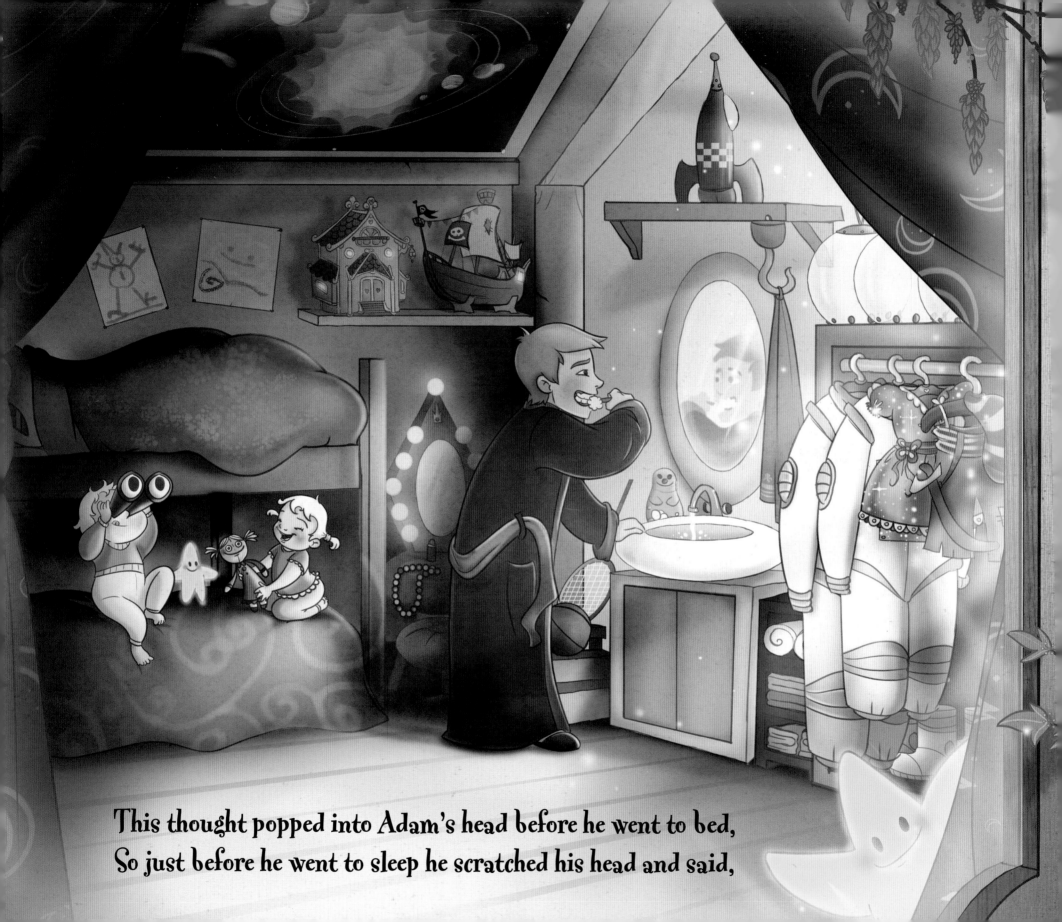

This thought popped into Adam's head before he went to bed,
So just before he went to sleep he scratched his head and said,

"Let's fly around the big blue world
that is so huge and round,
and find the most amazing thing
there is that can be found."

Fluff gave some help and flew them all up high into the sky
and found a most amazing thing that no one could deny.

"This is Rome's big Colosseum," said Harry, with surprise,
"This is where the Roman folks could not believe their eyes.
Gladiators fought with lions and chariots raced so fast,
Around this big arena that is so huge and vast."

"This is amazing," Adam said, "but let's go and find some more
Amazing things that can be found," then called Fluff with a roar.
Fluff arrived to Adam's call and beamed his big huge smile
then flew them to a Pharaohs' land near Egypt's river Nile.

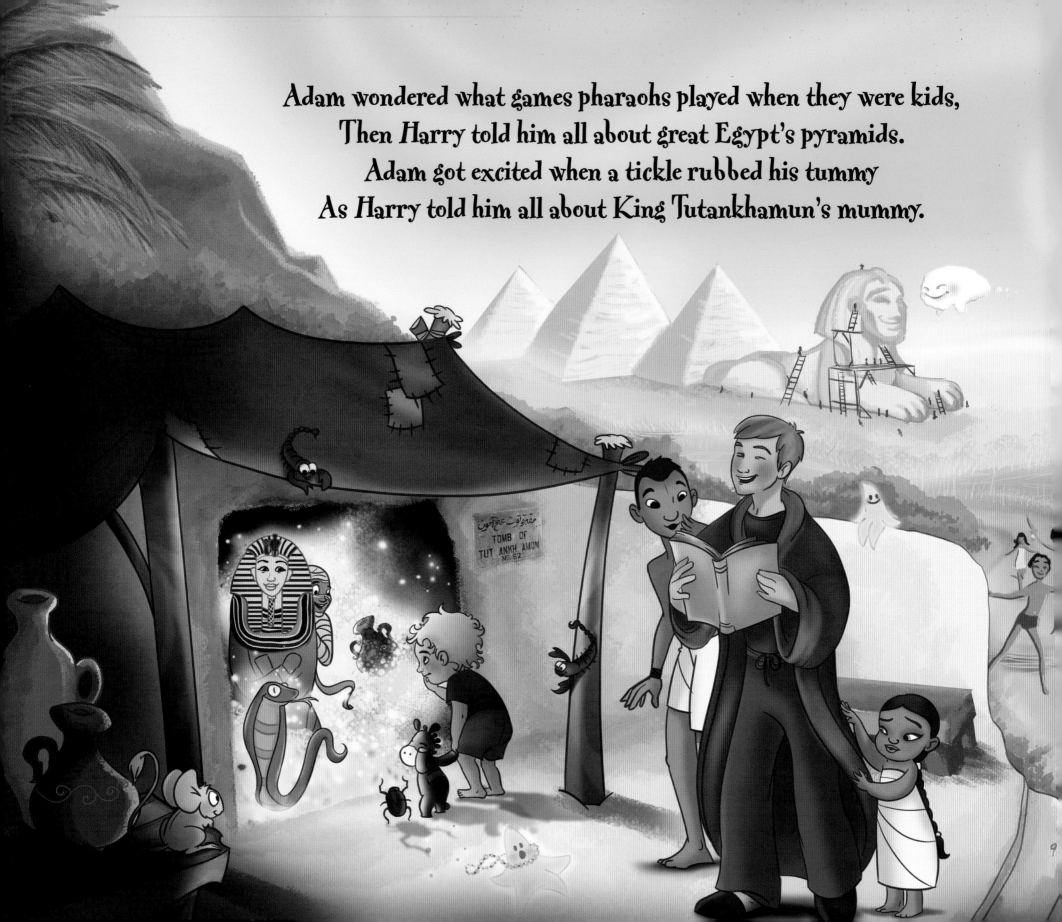

Adam wondered what games pharaohs played when they were kids,
Then Harry told him all about great Egypt's pyramids.
Adam got excited when a tickle rubbed his tummy
As Harry told him all about King Tutankhamun's mummy.

TOMB OF
TUT ANKH AMON
NO. 62

Locked away inside his tomb with all his jewels and gold,
Keeping guard of ancient secrets never to be told.
When Adam saw the mummy's face his heart began to race
"Fluff," he screamed, "this is scary, let's leave this spooky place."

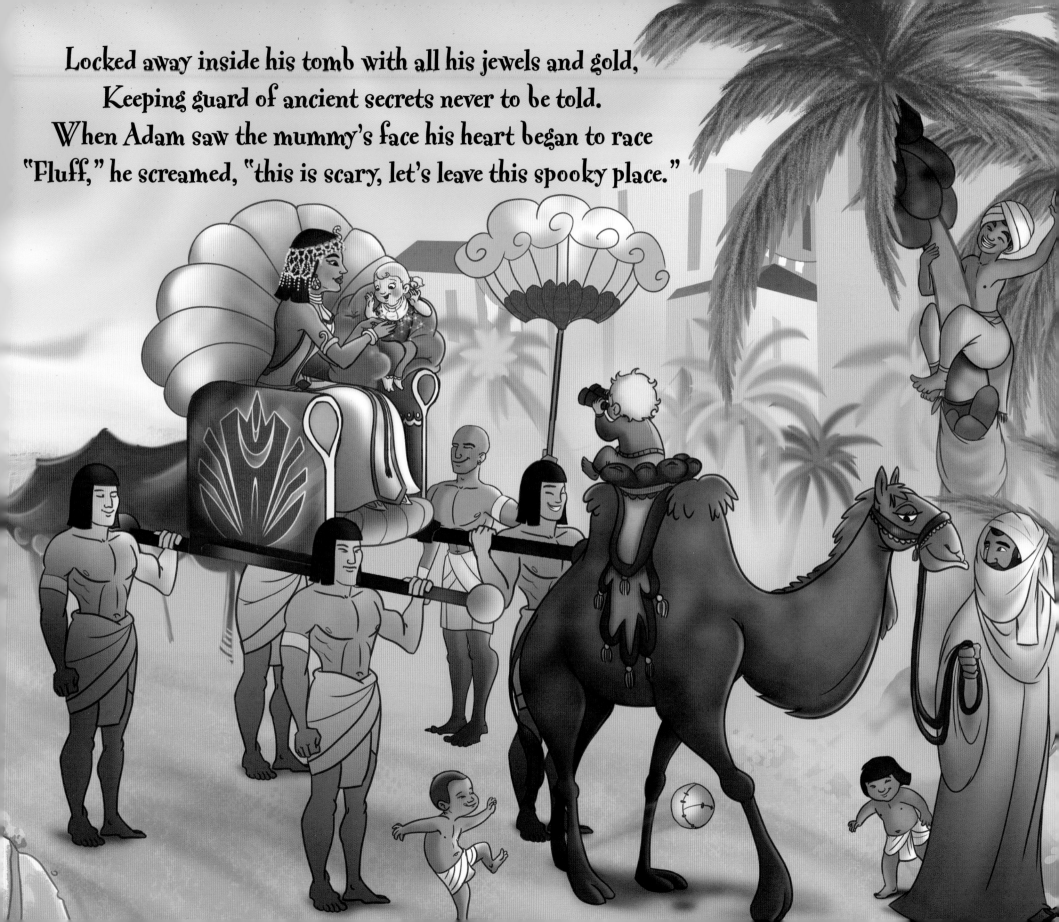

Fluff flew high into the sky
then landed at a tower,
When Adam saw how odd it looked he
laughed for half an hour.
He giggled and he wiggled at the
strangest thing he'd seen,
A tower with a bell on top
so funny it could lean.

The laughing made him hungry so he stopped to have some pizza,
Then Harry told him all about the leaning tower of Pisa.
"Whoever built this funny thing must really be so proud,
But funny leaning towers really should not be allowed."

Fluff flew the boys across the sky to a land of fairytales,
Where wizards cast their magic spells on dragons with long tails.
He landed at King Ludwig's castle high upon a hill
"I can't believe my eyes," said Adam, "this is such a thrill."

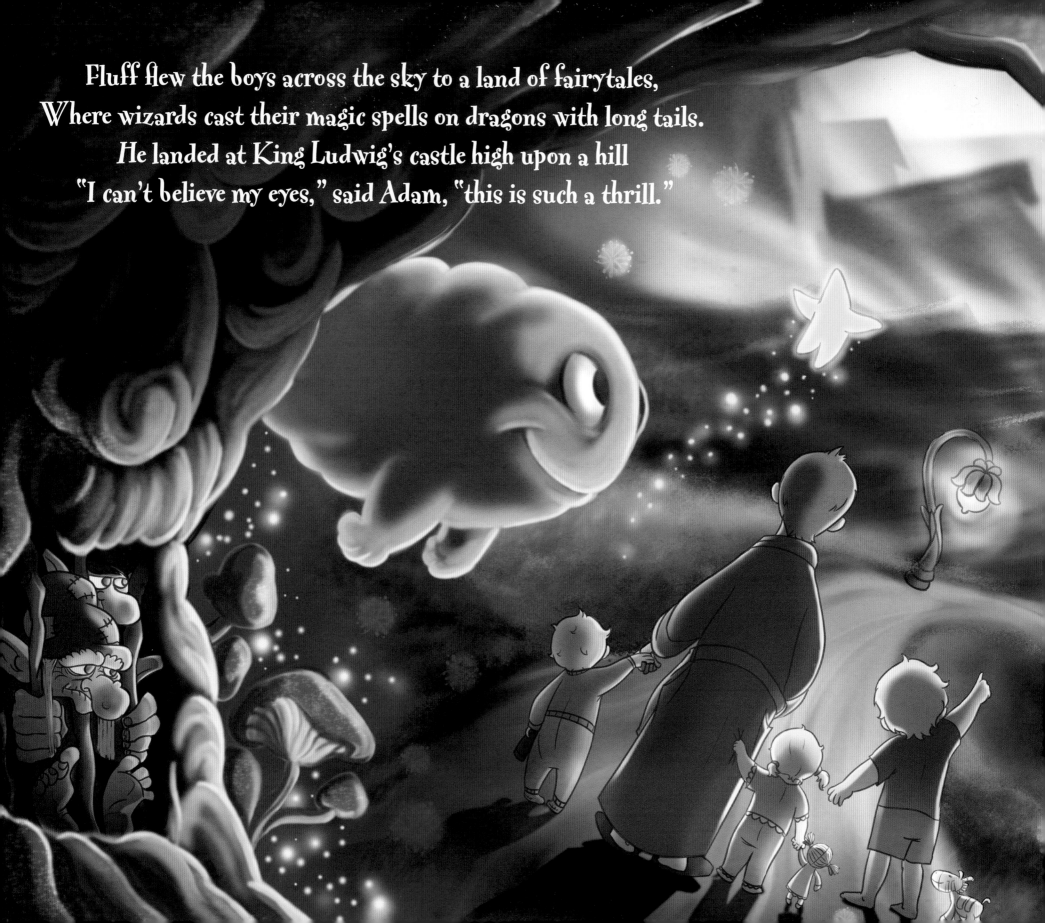

Trolls and goblins locked in dungeons deep down underground,
Kept there for safe keeping as a brave young prince is crowned.
Adam thought one day he might become a shining knight,
And slay a nasty dragon and then marry sweet Snow White.

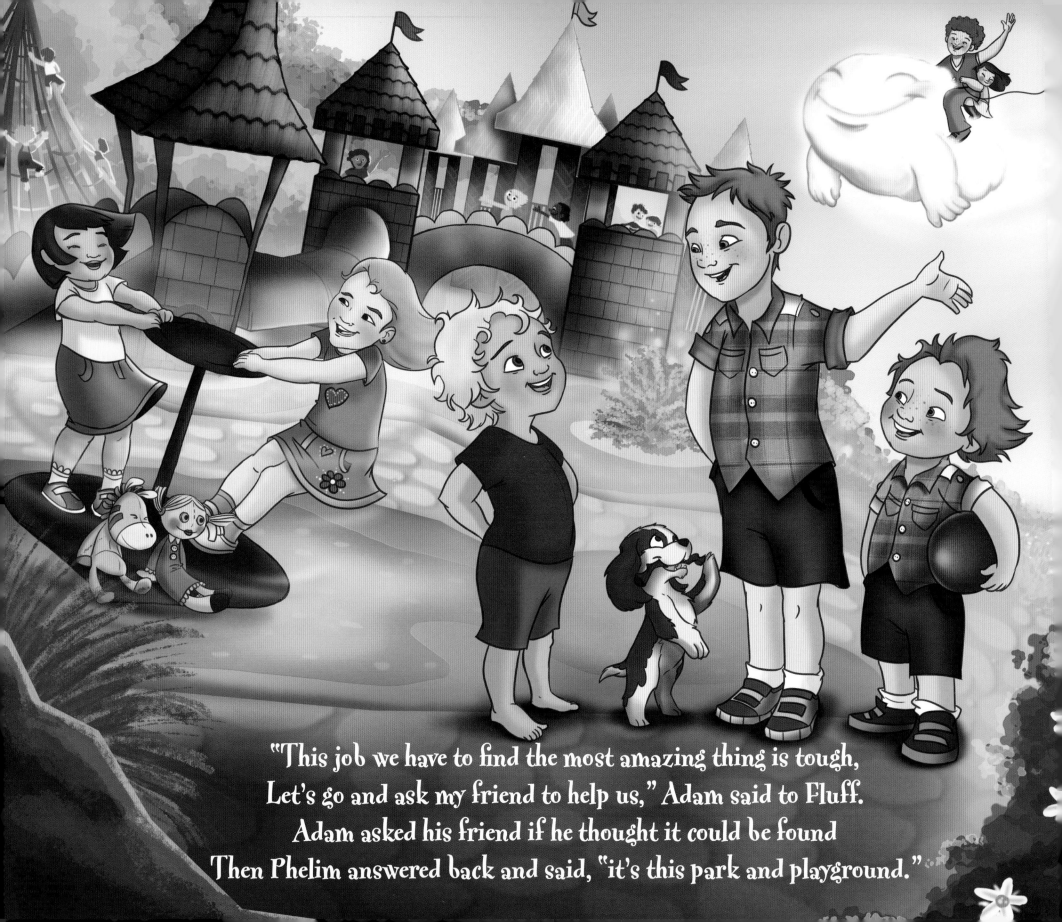

"This job we have to find the most amazing thing is tough,
Let's go and ask my friend to help us," Adam said to Fluff.
Adam asked his friend if he thought it could be found
Then Phelim answered back and said, "it's this park and playground."

I come here with my trusty dog and play fetch with a stick,
Then after swinging on the swings I eat mum's yum picnic."
"Cool!" said Adam, "but we have to find another if we can."
Then Fluff flew them to a palace built by Emperor Jahan.

"Adam we're so lucky," said Harry to his pal,
"This palace where true love lies is the famous Taj Mahal.
The Emperor loved his wife so much he built her this fine tomb,
And now they sleep forever side by side as bride and groom."
"It's time to leave the happy couple sleeping side by side,"
said Adam as he called Fluff back to bring them for a ride.

After flying all around the world Adam was not sure
He'd found the most amazing thing and wanted to look more.
But as the sun went off to sleep the moon began to rise,
Adam felt quite sleepy and began to rub his eyes.
"Oh no! it's time for bed," said Adam, "we can't look any more,"
So fluff Flew the gang back home right to their bedroom door.

Before they got into their beds, mum and dad came up to say
Good night to all the children in their very special way.
But Adam was a little sad as he really did not think
He'd found the most amazing thing and could not sleep a wink.
A thought then popped into his head that nearly made him roar,
"That's it," said Adam, "I can't believe I did not think of it before.
The most wonderful thing in this wonderful world is a cuddly family hug
We give to each other before we sleep as snug as a bug in a rug."

And with that thought in his little tired head
Adam fell fast asleep in his big comfy bed.
"I love you much more than the wonderful things
in this wonderful world of ours,
That is so wonderful when you're asleep
safe under bright twinkling stars."